DADDIES
All About the Work They Do

By Janet Frank
Updated by Margo Lundell
Illustrated by Paul Meisel

A GOLDEN BOOK • NEW YORK
Golden Books Publishing Company, Inc., Racine, Wisconsin 53404

What do daddies do all day?
They go to work to earn their pay.

They work in offices
and stores,

in factories
and out of doors.

Farmer daddies keep us fed.
They grow the wheat we need for bread.

Dads build rockets.

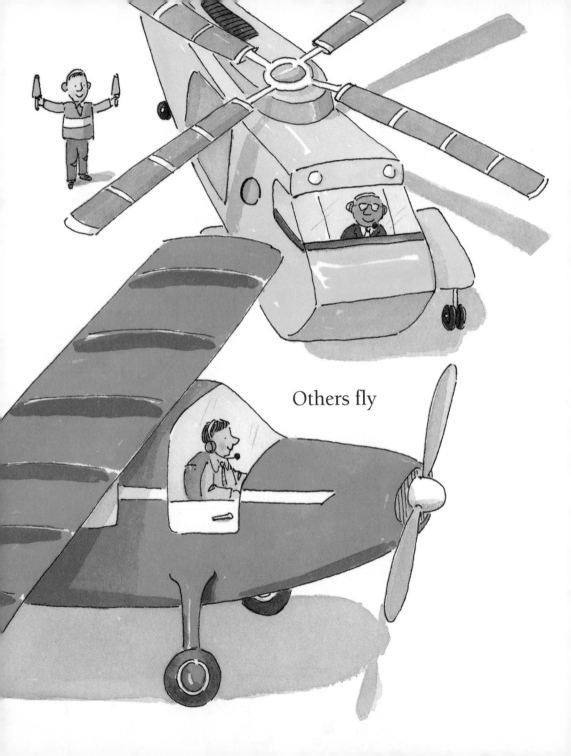

Others fly

or drive the trucks you see roll by.

Daddies fix the shoes we wear.

Barber daddies cut our hair.

Dads are sailors dressed in blue.

And daddies are policemen, too.

Daddies paint

and daddies sell.

Doctor daddies keep us well.

Daddies sit at desks and write

the books we read in bed at night.

A daddy might deliver mail.

Some teach science.

Some teach Braille.

Dads make steel

and daddies sing.
Dads do almost everything.

But when they've worked the whole
day through,
what do they really love to do?
By taxi, train, by car and bus,

daddies hurry home—to us!